The Lonely Princess

Written by Marie Ferraro

Illustrated by Domingo Zapata

From Marie:
To my Nana, Cristiana, who had room in her heart for everyone. This is for you.
To Mom, I am everything I am because of your love.

From Domingo:
To Dominga and Paul, you are the sunshine of my heart.

250 East 54th Street, Suite P2
New York, NY 10022
www.lightswitchlearning.com

Educators and Librarians, for a variety of teaching resources, visit www.lightswitchlearning.com.
Library of Congress Cataloging-in-Publication Data is available upon request.
Library of Congress Catalog Card Number pending.

ISBN: 978-1-68265-659-4

The text of this book is set in Din 1451.
Printed in China

There was a young princess named Cristiana, who lived in a castle with a gleaming golden tower. The Princess had beautiful silk dresses in every color of the rainbow. Her meals were brought to her on silver trays. She had everything a young girl might want, except for one thing.

The Princess had no mama or papa, so her heart was always heavy with loneliness.

The Princess's bedroom was at the very top of the castle's tower with windows that looked out in several directions. The shops and houses of the village were to the south. To the west were mountains capped with pure white snow, and to the east a deep blue river shimmered in the sun. But she liked to look north most of all.

Looking north at the edge of the ancient forest, the Princess could see a small house with a crooked roof. It was home to a young girl and her family.

Each afternoon, the Princess watched the young girl named Mia playing outside with a little grey mouse. The girl's dress was tattered, and she had neither toys nor even shoes. Whenever the Princess caught sight of the girl, her heart felt light and warm.

Every day, the Princess watched the girl
play until Mia's papa returned from working
in the woods and her mama opened the
door. When they went inside, the Princess's
heart would grow heavy again.

One Christmas Eve, the golden tower filled with the scents of baking and roasting. There would be both a great feast for the Princess the next day and a pile of finely wrapped gifts.

7

At her window, the Princess stared far up at the moon.

"Oh Moon, why am I sad when I have so much?" she asked.

"Oh Moon, grant me a wish that I become the woodcutter's daughter, even for one day."

The Princess did not know that at that very moment, the woodcutter's daughter was also making a wish upon the moon.

"Oh Moon," said Mia, "I have nothing of my own but my little mouse.

"Oh Moon, grant me a wish—that I am the princess for one day, with a red velvet dress and a crown of flowers."

"The wishes of one are the riches of others,"
the Moon then said to the Princess. "Mia longs to
be a princess."

"Oh Moon," said the Princess, "you say she
wishes to be me. But these clothes and riches do
not make me happy. I wish I could tell her."

12

"You can tell her," the Moon said.

But the Princess was afraid to speak to anyone because she had not left the golden tower for so long. She sighed. Her wish would never come true.

Mia," said the Moon, "the castle is open to all. Anyone may visit with a gift."

"I am too poor to buy a gift," said Mia. "I cannot visit a princess with nothing to give."

"You do have something to give," said the Moon. "The Princess is very lonely. You can offer the gift of friendship."

Mia's eyes brightened. "Oh Moon, I will!" she replied.

Mia walked through the night, her feet wet with snow. The Moon lit her path with its radiant glow. At dawn, Mia arrived at the castle. She climbed the stairs of the tower. When the Princess saw Mia, her eyes went wide.

"Princess, my name is Mia," she said with a curtsy. "The Moon told me about you. Please don't be sad. I don't have much, but I can be your friend."

The Princess's eyes filled with tears as Mia took her hands.

"I must get home soon," Mia said. "Why don't you come?"

"Leave the golden tower?" the Princess asked.

"Yes, spend Christmas with my family. We have no feast, but Papa brings us slender branches, and Mama paints them white and makes them into a Christmas tree. It's not fancy, but it's always the prettiest Christmas tree in the kingdom!"

But Mia had not asked for anything herself.

"The Moon told me about you too, Mia," the Princess said. "I will go with you, but only if you accept this red velvet dress and crown of flowers."

"Oh, thank you!" Mia exclaimed, her eyes shining.

Soon, they were on their way, nestled under
a cozy blanket in the royal carriage.

As they arrived and climbed out of the carriage, the door of the house opened.

The Princess saw Mia's papa and mama, their faces beaming.

"I brought a friend," Mia said.

"You are very welcome here," said Mia's mama. "Come inside!"

As the Princess walked into the house, she saw a tree made of old branches painted a perfect pure-white.

"Oh!" the Princess exclaimed. "It truly is the prettiest Christmas tree in the kingdom!"

The Princess sent the coachman to fetch the royal feast. Then she sat by the fire, cuddling the little grey mouse and smiling into Mia's clear blue eyes.

And so, at that moment, the Princess knew the Moon had made her wish come true.

Here, in this small, simple home was true happiness.

She now had the gift of friendship and a loving family. Finally, she was able to share all she had been given as a princess.

Depth of Knowledge

DISCUSSION QUESTIONS

1. In what ways are the Princess and Mia alike? How are they different?

2. If you had to choose between having lots of things or having friends, which would you choose? Explain.

3. On page 6, the author writes that the Princess's heart would "grow heavy." What does that mean?

4. Why does the Princess talk to the moon on page 9? Why does Mia talk to the moon on page 10? Explain.

5. On page 13, the Princess thinks her wish will never come true. What has happened to make her think that?

6. Why does Mia walk through the night to get to the castle? What does she hope will happen?

7. Look at the illustration on page 15. What clues can you find that explain what Mia is feeling?

8. Mia likes to play with her little grey mouse. Having a pet is a big responsibility. What are some things you need to do to take care of a pet? Explain.

9. Why do Mia's parents welcome the Princess into their home?

10. What different feelings did you experience today? How are they similar to or different from the Princess's and Mia's feelings?

ACTIVITIES

1. Write a story about someone who doesn't have something that you have. How would you share what you have with that person?

2. Mia wishes to be a princess. Draw a picture that represents something you have wished for.

3. Write a poem describing a friend or member of your family. Describe everything you like about that person and the things you do together.

4. Imagine a person who has never spent a holiday with friends or family members. Make a holiday card inviting them to your home. Describe the things you might do together during the holidays.

5. Draw a picture that represents a tradition in your home.

GROUP ACTIVITY
Share Perspectives

- Pair up students in the class who don't know each other very well.

- Provide each pair with five questions to ask each other so that the two students can learn more about each other's perspectives and experiences.

- Have each student introduce his or her partner to the class, speaking as if he or she were actually the partner instead.

- Have each partner explain what he or she learned about the partner's perspectives and experiences in life.

Glossary

Ancient *(adjective)* very old *(p. 4)*

Beaming *(verb)* smiling happily *(p. 23)*

Capped *(verb)* to cover the top of something *(p. 3)*

Carriage *(noun)* a vehicle that's pulled by a horse *(p. 20)*

Coachman *(noun)* someone who drives a carriage *(p. 25)*

Crooked *(adjective)* not straight *(p. 4)*

Cuddling *(verb)* to hold close for comfort or warmth *(p. 25)*

Curtsy *(noun)* a way of greeting someone by placing one foot slightly behind the other and bending at the knees *(p. 17)*

Dawn *(noun)* the time of day when the sun rises *(p. 14)*

Fancy *(adjective)* expensive and pretty *(p. 17)*

Feast *(noun)* a big meal *(p. 7)*

Finely *(adverb)* carefully *(p. 7)*

Gleaming *(adjective)* shining brightly *(p. 1)*

Grant *(verb)* give *(p. 9)*

Longs *(verb)* to want something a lot *(p. 11)*

Nestled *(verb)* to lie down close to something else *(p. 20)*

Radiant *(adjective)* bright and shining *(p. 14)*

Roasting *(verb)* cooking *(p. 7)*

Royal *(adjective)* something that comes from a king or queen *(p. 20)*

Shimmered *(verb)* to shine with a light that seems to move *(p. 3)*

Sighed *(verb)* to let out a long, loud breath *(p. 13)*

Silk *(noun)* a smooth, soft, shiny cloth *(p. 1)*

Simple *(adjective)* plain *(p. 27)*

Slender *(adjective)* thin *(p. 17)*

Stared *(verb)* to look at something for a long time *(p. 9)*

Velvet *(noun)* a type of soft cloth *(p. 10)*

Woodcutter *(noun)* a person whose job is to cut wood *(p. 9)*

Acknowledgments

From Marie

To my husband, you are the beginning of my forever.
I love you.

To Domingo Zapata, few can see beauty
in everything and leave beauty everywhere they go.
Thank you for your gifts.

To my dad, thank you for always inspiring
and believing in me.

To my son, my greatest reason,
you are walking sunshine. The stars await you.

To my Dmitri, your compassion for others is
unparalleled. The love you emanate
will change the world.

From Domingo

To Jill Zarin, thank you for always helping me
to grow as an artist and as a person!
This book exists because of you!